2/27/91

Dear Emily,
I hope you like
this book as much as
I do. I cant wait to
play with you!!
Love,
Collin ♡

2.8.05

A FAIRY
WENT A-MARKETING

by Rose Fyleman
illustrated by Jamichael Henterly

E. P. DUTTON · NEW YORK

for Ann Marie and Lael Lupine

Permission to reprint "A Fairy Went A-Marketing," from *Fairies and Chimneys* by Rose Fyleman, is gratefully acknowledged. Copyright 1918, 1920 by George H. Doran Co. Reprinted by permission of Doubleday & Company, Inc. and The Society of Authors as the literary representative of the Estate of Rose Fyleman.

Illustrations copyright © 1986 by Jamichael Henterly

Library of Congress Cataloging in Publication Data

Fyleman, Rose, 1877-1957.
A fairy went a-marketing.

Originally appeared in *Punch*, 1918.
Summary: A kindly fairy uses her purchases only for
a short time, then releases them for their own good
or the good of others.
1. Children's poetry, English.   [1. Fairies—Poetry.
2. English poetry]   I. Henterly, Jamichael, ill.
II. Title.
PR6011.Y5F35   1986   821'.912   86-4468
ISBN 0-525-44258-8

Published in the United States by E. P. Dutton,
a division of NAL Penguin Inc.
2 Park Avenue, New York, N.Y. 10016

Published simultaneously in Canada by
Fitzhenry & Whiteside Limited, Toronto

Designer: Isabel Warren-Lynch

Printed in Hong Kong by South China Printing Co.
First Edition   COBE   10 9 8 7 6 5 4 3 2

A fairy went a-marketing—
she bought a little fish;

she put it in a crystal bowl
upon a golden dish.

An hour she sat in wonderment
and watched its silver gleam,

and then she gently took it up
and slipped it in a stream.

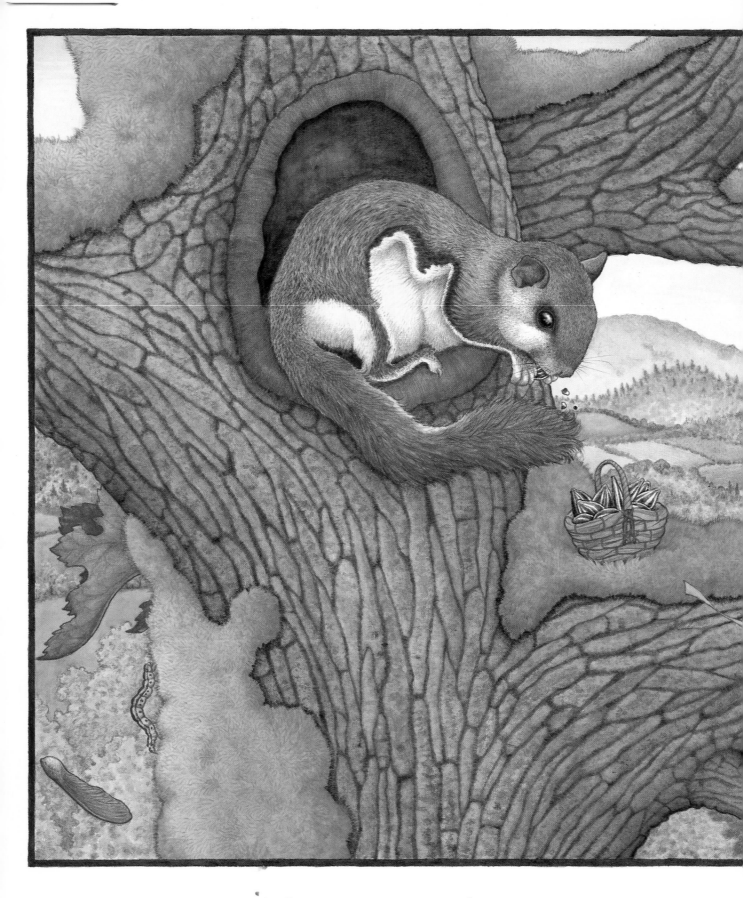

A fairy went a-marketing—
she bought a colored bird;

it sang the sweetest, shrillest song
that ever she had heard.

She sat beside its painted cage
and listened half the day,

and then she opened wide the door
and let it fly away.

A fairy went a-marketing—
she bought a winter gown

all stitched about with gossamer
and lined with thistledown.

She wore it all the afternoon
with prancing and delight,

then gave it to a little frog
to keep him warm at night.

A fairy went a-marketing—
she bought a gentle mouse

Corona

to take her tiny messages,
to keep her tiny house.

All day she kept its busy feet
pit-patting to and fro,

and then she kissed its silken ears,
thanked it, and let it go.